# THE GREAT P...
## SECRET...

Carmel Reilly  Mykel Rugers

Nelson CENGAGE Learning

Australia • Brazil • Japan • Korea • Mexico • Singapore • Spain • United Kingdom • United States

# NELSON
## CENGAGE Learning

**The Great Pharaoh's Secret Box**

Text: Carmel Reilly
Illustrations: Mykel Rugers
Editor: Vanessa Pellatt
Design: Jennifer Warwick
Series design: James Lowe
Production controller: Lisa Porter
Reprint: Siew Han Ong

**Fast Forward Independent Texts**
**Level 24**

Text © 2009 Cengage Learning Australia Pty Limited
Illustrations © 2009 Cengage Learning Australia Pty Limited

**Copyright Notice**
This Work is copyright. No part of this Work may be reproduced, stored in a retrieval system, or transmitted in any form or by any means without prior written permission of the Publisher. Except as permitted under the Copyright Act 1968, for example any fair dealing for the purposes of private study, research, criticism or review, subject to certain limitations. These limitations include: Restricting the copying to a maximum of one chapter or 10% of this book, whichever is greater; Providing an appropriate notice and warning with the copies of the Work disseminated; Taking all reasonable steps to limit access to these copies to people authorised to receive these copies; Ensuring you hold the appropriate Licences issued by the Copyright Agency Limited ("CAL"), supply a remuneration notice to CAL and pay any required fees.

ISBN 978 0 17 017997 3
ISBN 978 0 17 017899 0 (set)

**Cengage Learning Australia**
Level 7, 80 Dorcas Street
South Melbourne, Victoria Australia 3205
Phone: 1300 790 853

**Cengage Learning New Zealand**
Unit 4B Rosedale Office Park
331 Rosedale Road, Albany, North Shore NZ 0632
Phone: 0508 635 766

For learning solutions, visit **cengage.com.au**

Printed in China by 1010 Printing International Ltd
2 3 4 5 6 7 15

# THE GREAT PHARAOH'S SECRET BOX

Carmel Reilly  Mykel Rugers

## Contents

| | | |
|---|---|---|
| Chapter 1 | **Bored** | 4 |
| Chapter 2 | **The Secret Box** | 8 |
| Chapter 3 | **A Strange Feeling** | 14 |
| Chapter 4 | **Vanishing Act** | 18 |
| Chapter 5 | **The Professor** | 20 |

# BORED

It was the middle of the school holidays and Alex was bored. She'd finished all the mystery books and all the weird and wonderful history books in her local library.

Now she had no idea how she was going to fill the rest of her time.

"There's a show about ancient Egypt at the museum," observed her mum.
"Why don't you go and have a look?"

Alex's eyes lit up. "Oh cool!" she said. "Great idea, Mum. You know how I love all that stuff – especially the mummies."

The Great Pharaoh's Secret Box

Alex was surprised to find that it was really quiet in the museum. She had almost the whole place to herself.

She entered the ancient Egypt display room and started reading the information on how the pyramids were built.

*Bored*

Alex began peering into the glass cases. She examined the jewellery and the bowls and was impressed by their beauty. Moving away from the bowls, she saw a glass case in the very centre of the room.

"What's this?" she cried, as she took a step towards it.

"That is the Great Pharaoh's secret box," said a voice behind her.

## CHAPTER 2

# THE SECRET BOX

Alex spun around to see an old man standing nearby.

"The Great Pharaoh," she repeated. "Isn't he …"

"Famous?" said the old man. "Yes, he was the one whose tomb was robbed. That box was one of the things that was taken."

*The Secret Box*

"The legend says that the box held something so precious that the Pharaoh wanted to keep it by his side at all times," the elderly man told her.

Alex stared at the box. "I've heard that horrible things happened to the men who robbed the Great Pharaoh's tomb."

"Oh yes!" the old man said. "They suffered terrible consequences for stealing from the tomb's chambers."

*The Great Pharaoh's Secret Box*

"Soon after the treasure was taken, one of the robbers fell from his horse and was immediately killed," the old man continued. "Another went out for a walk one day and simply disappeared. And the last one was lost at sea. The robbers' families lost their homes and all their money."

*The Secret Box*

"Oh! How awful!" said Alex. "What happened to all the treasure?"

"No one knows," said the old man. "The stories suggest that the ghost of the pharaoh came back for it. The only thing that he's missing is this box. Some say he's still looking for a way to retrieve it."

Alex shuddered.

*The Great Pharaoh's Secret Box*

The old man gave Alex a funny smile.

"But of course, there's no such thing as ghosts. So we don't need to worry about that," he said, as he wandered off into another room.

The Secret Box

Alex anxiously looked around the room. It seemed too dark and too quiet now the old man had left.

She leaned forward to take a closer look at the box. Something about it made her feel even more nervous. She decided to ignore it and go back to the rest of the show.

# A STRANGE FEELING

There were so many things to see that Alex needed a break from looking at them, so she went upstairs for a cup of tea.

But as she sat looking out over the busy street, she had a strange feeling.
There was something very odd about that man downstairs.

"Of course!" cried Alex, leaping up and almost knocking her cup off the table.

*A Strange Feeling*

Alex ran down the stairs two by two and burst through the door. She ran back to where the secret box was on show. Even before she got close to the glass case, she could see that the box was missing.

"No!" she yelled. "No!"

*The Great Pharaoh's Secret Box*

The security guard rushed in from the next room.

"The Great Pharaoh's secret box has been taken!" Alex shrieked at him.

The guard stared at the case and then back at Alex. "But there's no broken glass," he said. "The case doesn't even look damaged."

*A Strange Feeling*

"Well, of course not," snapped Alex. "He wouldn't need to break the glass!"

"Who are you talking about?" the guard said. He looked worried.

Just then, she looked up and thought she saw the old man two rooms away, walking around a corner.

"Stop!" she called, running after him.

# CHAPTER 4

# VANISHING ACT

When Alex got to the room, the old man had vanished! She looked around, but there were no other rooms that he could have gone into.

How could he have escaped?

Then, she saw a door painted the same colour as the wall and marked "Staff Only".

*Vanishing Act*

The guard appeared as Alex was trying to force open the door.

"What are you doing?" he yelled.

"Looking for the person who took the box," said Alex. "I think he went in here."

"Well …" the guard started to say.

Just at that moment, the door opened. Standing there was a shape that looked like a mummy!

# THE PROFESSOR

"That's him!" screeched Alex, pointing at the shape. "That's him!"

"Yes, it is him," said the guard, looking a bit puzzled. "It's the professor."

The mummy-like shape stepped into the light and Alex could see straightaway that it was the old man.

"The professor?" she asked, staring at him. "But … you took the box!"

The professor laughed. "I'm in charge of the ancient Egypt collection," he said. "I wasn't stealing the box. I noticed the lid had come loose when we were talking before. I took it to the workshop to be repaired. Now I'm returning it."

"Oh, I'm sorry," said Alex, looking extremely embarrassed.

"By the way," Alex said as they walked back to the ancient Egypt display, "I forgot to ask what the box contained that was so special to the Great Pharaoh?"

"It was said to have held his spirit," the professor smiled.

Alex and the guard watched the professor put the box back in the case.

"He loves that ancient Egyptian stuff," whispered the guard. "I've heard he's been looking after the collection for years and years. In fact, some people can't remember a time when he wasn't around."

The Professor

*The Great Pharaoh's Secret Box*

"Nice to meet you," said the professor. "I hope you enjoyed the show!"

The professor waved goodbye to Alex and the guard as he left the room.

"Oh," the guard continued, "and he's got just the right name for the job too."

"What's that?" asked Alex.

"Professor Ferro."

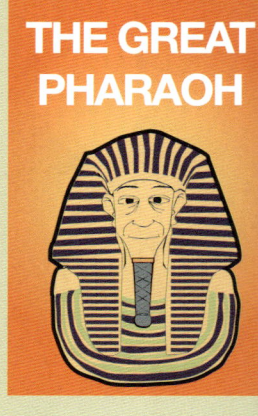

24